A Perfect Day

Sarah S. Brannen

Philomel Books

PHILOMEL BOOKS
An imprint of Penguin Random House LLC, New York

First published in the United States of America by Philomel,
an imprint of Penguin Random House LLC, 2020.

Visit us online at penguinrandomhouse.com

Library of Congress Cataloging-in-Publication Data is available.

Manufactured in China by RR Donnelley Asia Printing Solutions LTD.

ISBN 9781984812841

1 3 5 7 9 10 8 6 4 2

Edited by Talia Benamy.   Design by Jennifer Chung.   Text set in Highlander ITC Std.
The art was done in watercolor on 300 lb Arches Bright White cold press paper.

In memory of my perfect mother,
Barbara Brannen

Blue sky, gentle breeze!
Warm sun, cool feet!

It's a perfect day.

It's not perfect.

What do you mean
it's not perfect?

I see a cloud.

It's a pretty cloud.

There's a smelly old boat
right over there.

I like the boat.

This rock is slippery.
And it's covered with barnacles.

Fine! It's not perfect.
I'm going to find a better rock.

Warm sun, cool feet!
No crabs.

This is perfect.

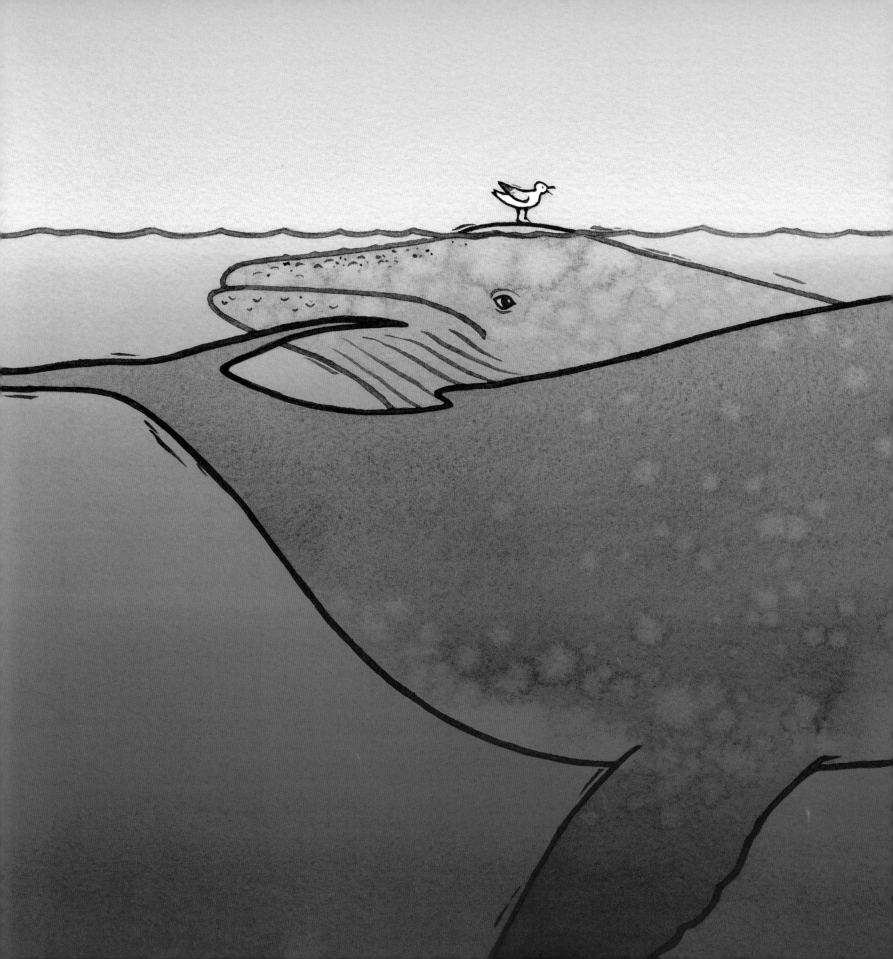

It's not perfect.

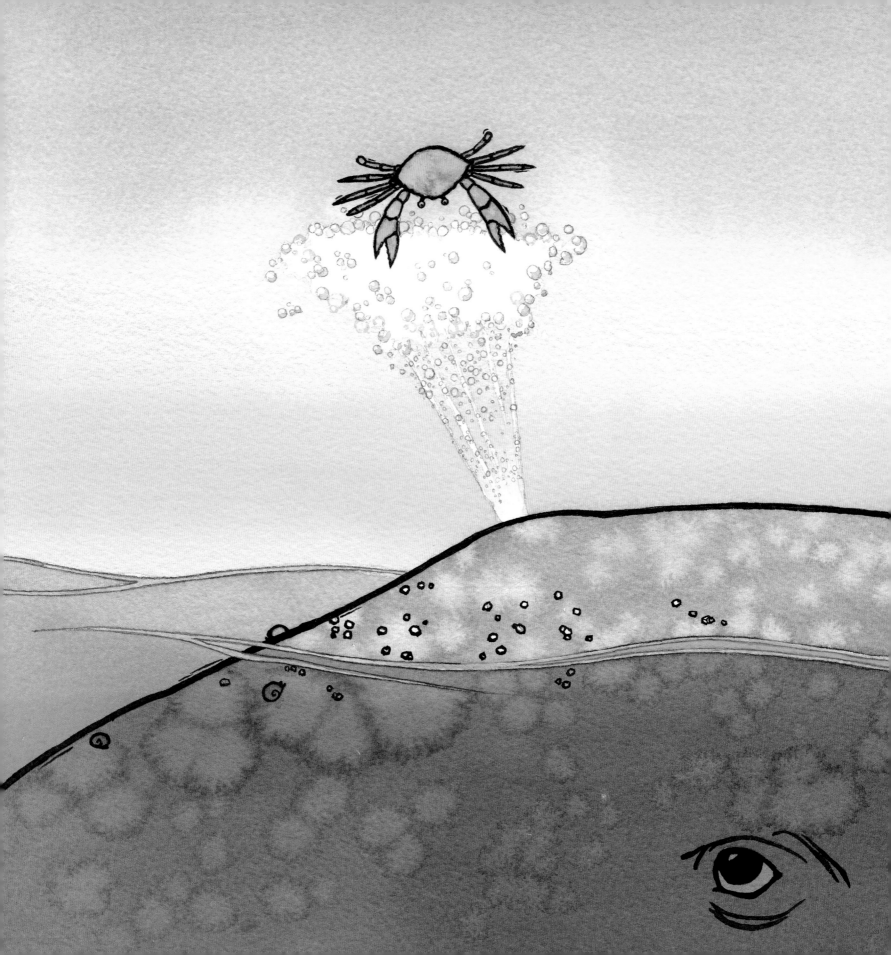

Setting sun, cool breeze!
Blue water, and a friend to share it all.
What a perfect day.

It's not perfect.

But it's good enough.